Dear Parent:

Congratulations! Your child is taking the first steps on an exciting journey. The destination? Independent reading!

STEP INTO READING® will help your child get there. The program offers five steps to reading success. Each step includes fun stories and colorful art. There are also Step into Reading Sticker Books, Step into Reading Math Readers, Step into Reading Phonics Readers, Step into Reading Write-In Readers, and Step into Reading Phonics Boxed Sets—a complete literacy program with something to interest every child.

Learning to Read, Step by Step!

Ready to Read   Preschool–Kindergarten
• big type and easy words • rhyme and rhythm • picture clues
For children who know the alphabet and are eager to begin reading.

Reading with Help   Preschool–Grade 1
• basic vocabulary • short sentences • simple stories
For children who recognize familiar words and sound out new words with help.

Reading on Your Own   Grades 1–3
• engaging characters • easy-to-follow plots • popular topics
For children who are ready to read on their own.

Reading Paragraphs   Grades 2–3
• challenging vocabulary • short paragraphs • exciting stories
For newly independent readers who read simple sentences with confidence.

Ready for Chapters   Grades 2–4
• chapters • longer paragraphs • full-color art
For children who want to take the plunge into chapter books but still like colorful pictures.

STEP INTO READING® is designed to give every child a successful reading experience. The grade levels are only guides. Children can progress through the steps at their own speed, developing confidence in their reading, no matter what their grade.

Remember, a lifetime love of reading starts with a single step!

For brave Ramona and her heroic brother, Leo
—A.J.

Step into Reading, Random House, and the Random House colophon are registered trademarks
of Random House, Inc.

Visit us on the Web!
StepIntoReading.com
randomhouse.com/kids

Educators and librarians, for a variety of teaching tools, visit us at
RHTeachersLibrarians.com

ISBN: 978-0-7364-2887-3 (trade) — ISBN: 978-0-7364-8114-4 (lib. bdg.)

Printed in the United States of America   10 9 8 7 6 5 4 3

Disney · PIXAR

BRAVE

OH, BROTHER!

By Apple Jordan

Illustrated by Studio IBOIX
and Maria Elena Naggi

Random House 🏠 New York

This is Merida.

She is a brave princess.

Merida's mother
is the queen.

Merida's father
is the king.

These are Merida's
three brothers.

They are triplets.

The triplets have fun!

They play games.

The triplets listen
to stories.

13

The triplets climb
on their dad.

The queen
loves her family.

The queen eats
a piece of cake.
It has a magic spell
in it.

The queen turns
into a bear!

The triplets
are not afraid.
They know the bear
is their mother.

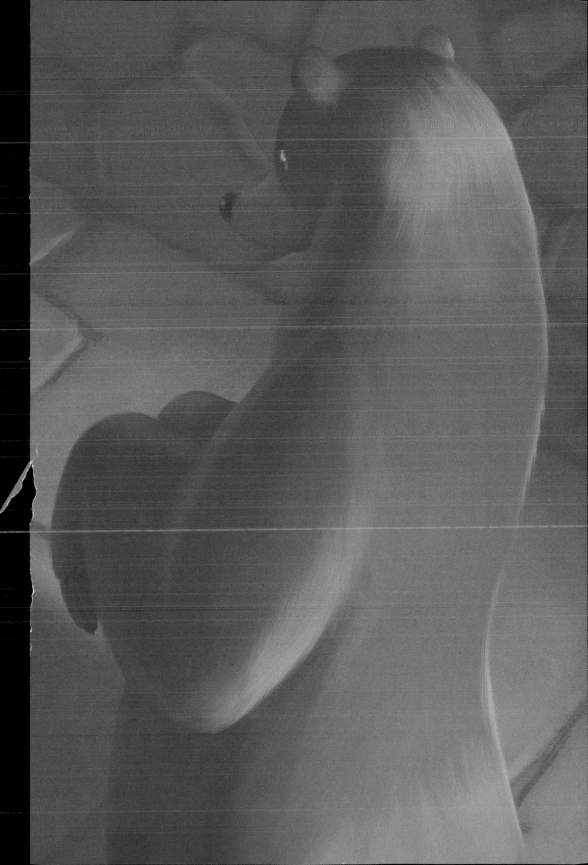

The triplets eat
the magic cake,
too.

Oh, no!

The triplets turn into bear cubs!

The cubs scare a maid.

The cubs ride
with Merida.

They have to break
the magic spell!

Merida and the cubs arrive just in time!

Merida protects
their mother.

The queen
is still a bear.

Merida hugs her.
The spell is broken!

Merida and her brothers
are very brave.